LOUDMOUTH
George and the Fishing Trip

LOUDMOUTH
George and the Fishing Trip

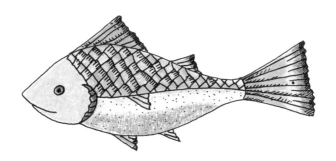

Nancy Carlson

PUFFIN BOOKS

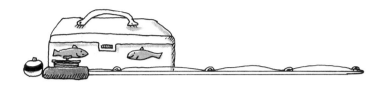

to Maddie Simons
because of her encouragement and energy

PUFFIN BOOKS

Viking Penguin Inc., 40 West 23rd Street, New York, New York 10010, U.S.A.
Penguin Books Ltd, Harmondsworth, Middlesex, England
Penguin Books Australia Ltd, Ringwood, Victoria, Australia
Penguin Books Canada Limited, 2801 John Street, Markham, Ontario, Canada L3R 1B4
Penguin Books (N.Z.) Ltd, 182–190 Wairau Road, Auckland 10, New Zealand

First published by Carolrhoda Books, Inc., 1983
Published in Picture Puffins 1985

Library of Congress Cataloging in Publication Data
Carlson, Nancy L.   Loudmouth George and the fishing trip.
Summary: Loudmouth George, a rabbit who brags about
catching the biggest fish even though he had never been
fishing, is embarrassed by the size of the fish he
finally does catch.
1. Children's stories, American.   [1. Rabbits—
Fiction.   2. Animals—Fiction.   3. Fishing—Fiction.
4. Pride and vanity—Fiction]   I. Title.
PZ7.C21665Lo 1985   [E]   84-18119 ISBN 0-14-050508-3

Printed in U.S.A.
by General Offset, Jersey City, New Jersey

George was always bragging.

According to him, he ran the fastest,

and he ate the biggest pizzas,

and he read the thickest books.

So when Harriet told him she was going fishing on Saturday, of course George bragged that he caught the biggest fish.

"If you're such a good fisherman," said Harriet, "why don't you come with us?"

"I'd better not," said George. "I'd probably catch such a big fish, it would sink the boat."

Harriet didn't believe him for a minute.
When she got home, she asked her dad if
George could come with them on Saturday.

"Sure," said Dad. "I'll give his parents
a call."

"Guess what, George?" said George's
mother. "Harriet's father just called and
invited you to go fishing tomorrow. Won't
that be fun?"

Oh, no! thought George. Why did I brag so much? The biggest fish I ever caught was in the pet shop.

Early the next morning they were off to
the river.

"George, I brought an extra fishing rod
if you need it," said Harriet's mother.

"As a matter of fact, I do. You see, the last time I went fishing, I hooked this enormous fish. It was so big, it broke my fishing rod," George bragged.

At last they were out on the water.

"Here's a worm for your hook, George,"
said Harriet.

"I thought you'd fished before," said Harriet.

"Well, I have," George fibbed, "but we didn't use worms. We used other stuff."

So Harriet baited George's hook. Then they
sat ... and they sat ...

...and they sat. They sat for three hours, and no one got even a nibble.

"I think we'll call it a day," said Harriet's father. "The fish just aren't biting today."

Thank heaven, thought George as he started to reel in his line. Suddenly his bobber went down.

"You've got a fish, George!" yelled Harriet.

"Oh, wow!" said George. "Help! What do
I do?"

"I thought you were the great fisherman,"
said Harriet.

"Uh...uh...I guess I exaggerated a little
bit," George confessed. "Help me!"

"Keep reeling it in, George," Harriet told
him.

"It's the biggest fish ever!" yelled George.

"You almost have it, George," said Harriet.
"Just keep reeling."

"It's so big, it will bite my hand off,"
yelled George.

"Here it comes," said Harriet.
"Ooops," said George.

"Better throw it back, George," said Harriet. "It's too little to keep."

"Well, it felt big," said George.

Monday at school George told Ralph all about the fishing trip.

"I caught a fish, and it was this big," he said.

"How big, George?" said Harriet.
"Well, this big," said George.

"How big?"

"Well, maybe it was only this big," said George.

"But it sure put up a big fight!"

Ms. Coco Is Loco!

seem · idea · pretty · still · secret · think

Dan Gutman

Pictures by
Jim Paillot

HarperTrophy®
An Imprint of HarperCollins *Publishers*

Harper Trophy® is a registered trademark of HarperCollins Publishers.

Ms. Coco Is Loco!

Text copyright © 2007 by Dan Gutman

Illustrations copyright © 2007 Jim Paillot

All rights reserved. Printed in the United States of America.

No part of this book may be used or reproduced in any manner whatsoever without written permission except in the case of brief quotations embodied in critical articles and reviews. For information address HarperCollins Children's Books, a division of HarperCollins Publishers, 10 East 53rd Street, New York, NY 10022.

www.harpercollinschildrens.com

Library of Congress Cataloging-in-Publication Data is available.

ISBN-10: 0-06-114154-2 (lib. bdg.) – ISBN-13: 978-0-06-114154-6 (lib. bdg.)

ISBN-10: 0-06-114153-4 (pbk.) – ISBN-13: 978-0-06-114153-9 (pbk.)

❖

First Harper Trophy edition, 2007

13 OPM 20 19 18

To Emma

Contents

Chillin' at the School Store

My name is A.J. and I hate school.

The only cool part of Ella Mentry School is the school store. It's a little room near the office where they sell stuff. Mostly they have pencils and pens and junk like that. They never have anything useful, like skateboards or video games.

Still, it's cool to buy stuff when you're at school.

The school store is open in the morning before the bell rings. The only problem is, I spent all my allowance over the weekend on a new football because some kid stole mine. So I didn't even have a dime to buy anything at the school store. Bummer in the summer!

"Guess what I bought with my own money?" this girl with curly brown hair named Andrea Young whispered to her crybaby friend Emily. Knowing Andrea, it was probably an encyclopedia.

"What did you buy?" asked Emily.

"An encyclopedia!" Andrea said, all

excited. "It's an encyclopedia for kids!"

Ugh. Andrea loves reading and books and school and anything else that's boring. She keeps a dictionary on her desk so she can look up words and show everybody how much she knows. Andrea is like a human filing cabinet.

"You know what I'm going to do with my encyclopedia?" Andrea asked Emily.

Knowing Andrea, she would probably read the whole thing in *ABC* order so she would know everything in the world.

"I'm going to read it in *ABC* order," Andrea bragged. "If I finish one letter every day, by the end of the month I'll know *everything*! Won't that be cool?"

Yeah, cool like an oven. I wish a set of encyclopedias would fall on Andrea's head.

The bell rang and we all rushed to class. Our teacher, Miss Daisy, told us to put away our stuff and get ready for circle time. That's when we sit around in a circle, so it has the perfect name.

Suddenly the voice of the school secretary, Mrs. Patty, came over the loudspeaker.

"Miss Daisy, please send Andrea and A.J. to Ms. Coco's room."

"Oooooh!" my friend Ryan said. "A.J. and Andrea are going to Ms. Coco's room again. They must be in *love!*"

"When are you gonna get married?" asked my other friend Michael.

If those guys weren't my best friends, I would hate them.

National Poetry Month Is Dumb

Me and Andrea walked down the hall to Ms. Coco's room. She's the gifted and talented teacher at Ella Mentry School. That doesn't mean *she's* gifted and talented. It means she teaches *kids* who are gifted and talented.

Me and Andrea are the only ones in

Miss Daisy's class who are in the G and T program. Don't ask me how I got in. The only talents I have are burping the alphabet and making farting noises with my armpits. But we all had to take a dumb test, and afterward Ms. Coco decided I was gifted and talented.

I *hate* being gifted and talented. I don't want to be a gifted and talented nerd like Andrea.

"Guess what, Arlo?" Andrea asked, as we walked down the hall. She calls me by my real name because she knows I hate it.

"Your butt," I replied.

(Any time anyone says "Guess what?" you should always say "Your butt." That's

the first rule of being a kid.)

"I'm taking a speed-reading class after school, so I can read faster," Andrea bragged.

Andrea takes classes in *everything*. If they gave a class in blowing your nose, she would take that class so she could get better at it.

"Wow," I said, "it must be wonderful being *you*."

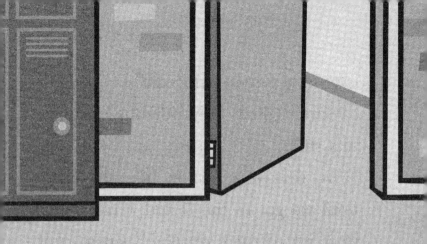

That's called sarcasm. It's when you say exactly the opposite of what you really mean. Sarcasm is fun, especially when you're talking to somebody you hate, like Andrea.

"Arlo, did you know that aardvarks eat termites?" Andrea said. "And did you know that ants rarely live more than sixty days?"

She must have been working on the

letter *A* in her encyclopedia.

"Sure," I lied. "Any dumbhead knows that stuff."

We walked a million hundred miles until we got to the G and T room. Ms. Coco wasn't there yet. She has posters of geniuses like Albert Einstein and Thomas Edison and the Beatles on the wall. And there are signs all over the place that say things like THINK!, CREATE!, and INVENT!

Finally Ms. Coco came running in. She wears tons of makeup on her face and her hair is always in place. I guess that's why she's late a lot. It must take a lot of time to make her look good.

"Hello!" she said to me and Andrea. "Do

you like yellow Jell-O? I can play the cello. Are you mellow?"

Ms. Coco is weird.

"Why are you talking in rhyme?" asked Andrea.

"Rhyme?" she said. "Is it a crime to talk in rhyme? I'd rather mime, but that takes more time."

"I get it!" Andrea said. "You're talking in rhyme because

it's April. It's National Poetry Month!"

National Poetry Month?! You've gotta be kidding me. Poetry gets a whole month? I wouldn't give poetry five minutes.

How come there's no National Skateboarding Month? Or National Video Games Month? It would be cool to go skateboarding and play video games all month instead of going to school.

"I love poetry," said Andrea, who loves everything teachers love. "I wrote a poem, and my mom put it on the refrigerator."

Andrea's mom is weird. If she puts poems on the refrigerator, she probably puts food on Andrea's notebooks.

"If you ask me, there should be a National Sit Around and Do Nothing

Month," I suggested.

"What a great idea, A.J.!" said Ms. Coco. "For homework I'd like each of you to write a poem. A.J., you can write yours about sitting around and doing nothing."

"But I was just joking!" I protested. "I hate poetry."

"Come on, A.J.," said Ms. Coco. "You're a poet and you don't even know it."

That is totally not fair. I wanted to sit around and do nothing, not write a *poem* about sitting around and doing nothing. Poetry is dumb. And now I had extra homework to do.

I wish I was in the U and U program— ungifted and untalented.

3

Sit Around and Do Nothing Month

The next morning at the school store, they were selling cool pens that light up. I counted the coins in my pocket—just enough money to buy lunch and nothing else. Bummer in the summer! I wish I brought my lunch from home, like I did in the good old days. Then I could use my lunch money to buy a pen. But if I brought lunch from home, I wouldn't have lunch money at all.

Well, anyway, all I had was enough money for lunch. And if I didn't eat lunch, I'd starve and die.

When I got to Miss Daisy's class, guess who poked his head in the door? Nobody! Because if you poked your head in a door, it would hurt. But Mr. Klutz poked his head in the door*way*. He is our principal, and he has no hair. Mr. Klutz's head is so shiny, you can *see* yourself in it. He must polish it or something.

Mr. Klutz is nuts.

"I have exciting news!" he said.

"Mr. Klutz said he has an exciting nose," I whispered to Neil Crouch, who we call Neil the nude kid even though he wears clothes.

"April is National Poetry Month!" said Mr. Klutz. "I thought of a great way to celebrate. If the students of Ella Mentry School write a thousand poems in April, I'll invite a real live poet to visit us. Isn't that exciting?"

"Yes!" yelled all the girls.

"No!" yelled all the boys.

A real live poet? I thought poets all died a long time ago.

"How about five hundred poems?" Michael asked.

"One thousand poems," Mr. Klutz said. "That's my final offer. Deal or no deal?"

"Deal!" yelled all the girls.

"No deal!" yelled all the boys.

Mr. Klutz loves challenging us to see what we can accomplish.

After he left, it was time for me and Andrea to go to Ms. Coco's room.

"Arlo, did you know that a beaver can hold its breath for five minutes?" Andrea asked as we walked down the hall. "And that bats sleep upside down in trees?"

Ugh. She must have finished the letter *B* in her encyclopedia.

"Sure," I lied. "Any dumbhead knows that stuff."

Ms. Coco came running in just as we reached the G and T room.

"Sorry I'm late," she said. "I had to fix my hair."

"Why, was it broken?" I asked.

"That's mean!" said Andrea.

"I think it's clever," said Ms. Coco. "To fix hair is to comb it, and you fix a machine when it breaks. A.J. thought creatively. That's why I selected him for the gifted and talented program."

"Thank you!" I said, and then I stuck my tongue out at Andrea.

"I'm so excited about National Poetry Month!" said Ms. Coco. "Did you two write your homework poems?"

"I did!" Andrea said, all excited. "My poem is called 'The Happy Hippo.' I worked on it all night."

Andrea loves animals. She read her

poem about some hippos that have a dumb tea party. It was totally lame.

"Lovely," said Ms. Coco when Andrea finished. "Let's hear your poem, A.J."

So I read my poem:

"I like to sit 'round and do nothing.
Just sit and do nothing at all.
I don't want to talk. I don't want to walk.
I don't want to play with a ball.
I don't want to eat or play with my feet
Or work up a sweat or fly in a jet.
If I could just sit and do nothing
Just sit there and clear my head
I'd be the happiest person
Except that, of course, I'd be dead."

I wasn't sure if Ms. Coco would like the ending or not. Teachers don't usually go for dead stuff. But when I looked up, there were tears running down her cheeks.

"That's the saddest poem I've ever heard!" she said, grabbing a tissue to wipe her face.

"Huh?" I said.

"A.J., your poem was simple, yet it was so moving. So honest. So free."

I didn't know what she was talking about. It was just a dumb poem. I wrote it in five minutes during the commercials while I watched TV.

"What about *my* poem?" asked Andrea.

"Yours was nice too, Andrea," said Ms. Coco. Then she took another tissue and started crying again.

Miss Smarty Pants Know-It-All crossed her arms and looked all mad. I guess she was angry because Ms. Coco liked my poem better than her dumb hippo poem.

Well, nah-nah-nah boo-boo on her.

Shakespeare Was a Dumbhead

When I got to school the next day, there was a big NATIONAL POETRY MONTH tote board on the front lawn. It said the kids of Ella Mentry School wrote two hundred poems already!

I didn't get it. I mean, I could see writing lots of poems if we were going to get a chocolate party or a video games night or something cool. But to have a poet visit our school? No thanks.

After we pledged the allegiance, Miss Daisy said our homework for April was to write one poem every day. Ms. Coco was going to publish a

National Poetry Month

National Poetry Month book with some of our best poems in it.

"Isn't that exciting?" Miss Daisy asked.

"Yes!" yelled all the girls.

"No!" yelled all the boys. Just the thought of writing something every day made me wrinkle up my nose like I smelled something bad.

"What's the matter, A.J.?" asked Miss Daisy.

"I hate poetry," I said.

"'Hate' is not a nice word," Miss Daisy said. "You shouldn't say that."

"Then I strongly dislike poetry," I said. "I despise poetry. I detest it. I loathe it. I—"

"That's enough, A.J.," said Miss Daisy.

Just then, a poem popped into my brain:

I hate poetry.
Poetry is dumb.
It's hard to write poems
When you're chewing gum.

Genius poems like that come into my brain all the time. I can't stop them! I guess that's why I'm in the gifted and talented program.

I was going to think up another verse, but it was time for me and Andrea to go see Ms. Coco again.

"Arlo, did you know that camels have

three eyelids?" Andrea said as we walked to the G and T room. "And cats see six times better than humans at night. And all clams start out as males, but some of them become females later."

Ugh. She must have finished the letter *C* in her encyclopedia.

"Any dumbhead knows that stuff," I said.

When we got to Ms. Coco's room, she was crying again. Nobody had even read her a poem. I figured Ms. Coco's dog must have died or something.

"What's wrong?" asked Andrea.

"When I woke up this morning, I saw the most beautiful sunrise," Ms. Coco said. "I don't know what came over me. It just made me want to cry."

Man, that lady will cry over *anything*. She's worse than Emily.

"What's so sad about a sunrise?" I asked.

"Wouldn't a beautiful sunrise make *you* cry, A.J.?" Ms. Coco asked.

"No," I said.

"A sunrise could make *me* cry," said Andrea, who always agrees with everything grown-ups say.

"I might cry if I woke up and the sun *didn't* rise," I said.

Then the weirdest thing in the history of the world happened. Ms. Coco started singing!

"'Feelings,'" she sang, "'nothing more than feelings . . .'"

Ms. Coco is loco!

Andrea must have known the song too, because she started singing along with Ms. Coco. It was horrible. Neither of them is gifted or talented when it comes to singing, believe me. I thought I was gonna die.

Finally, they finished the song.

"A.J., I want you to explore your feelings," said Ms. Coco. "It will make you a better poet."

"Boys don't have feelings," Andrea said. "They

just like to play sports and punch each other."

"Of course boys have feelings," said Ms. Coco. "They just hide them sometimes. You have feelings, don't you, A.J.?"

"Sure I do," I said. "The other day some kid stole my football, and I felt like punching him."

Andrea rolled her eyes.

"I have an idea," Ms. Coco said. "Let's write poems about feelings!"

Ugh! What is her problem? Every time I say anything about *anything*, Ms. Coco makes me write a poem about it.

She gave us each a piece of paper and a pencil. I didn't have any genius ideas.

So this is what I wrote:

My feelings are written on the ceiling.
But the paint is peeling off the ceiling.
So my feelings are not that revealing.
It's hard to have no feelings,
But I'm dealing.

At that point, I ran out of words that rhymed with "feelings," so I stopped writing.

"You know, A.J.," Ms Coco said as she took a book off her shelf, "poems don't *have* to rhyme."

"They don't?"

"No," Ms. Coco said. "Listen to this."

And she read a poem from the book:

"To gild refined gold, to paint the lily,
To throw a perfume on the violet,
To smooth the ice, or add another hue
Unto the rainbow, or with taper-light"

Ms. Coco sighed.

"That was beautiful!" said Andrea. "Who wrote it?"

"William Shakespeare," replied Ms. Coco.

"Who's he?" I asked.

"Only the most famous writer in the world!" Andrea said.

"Well, he was a dumbhead," I said.

"That poem made no sense at all."

"Poems don't always have to make sense," said Ms. Coco. "Sometimes they just paint a word picture."

What?! Poems don't have to rhyme *and* they don't even have to make sense? That just proves my point—poetry is dumb. You could put a bunch of words in *any* old order and call them a poem.

Suddenly I got the greatest idea in the history of the world.

But I'm not going to tell you what it was.

Okay, okay, I'll tell you. But you'll have to read the next chapter.

Ha-ha. In your face!

My Secret Poetry Writing System

I knew you'd keep reading.

When I got home, I looked through my closet for the big box of spelling flash cards my grandma gave me for my birthday.

You know what flash cards are, right? Each card has one word on it. You're supposed to use the cards to help you remember how to spell. I used them to build a tower instead. It was cool. Then I put them in the back of my closet.

I opened the box and took out a stack of cards. I figured if poems don't have to rhyme, then it's easy to write one. And if poems don't even have to make sense, you can just take any words and put them in any order and call it a poem.

So I took the stack of flash cards and threw it up in the air.

The cards flew all over the place and fluttered to the floor. I scooped up a bunch of them and wrote the words down in order:

Underground idea still afraid,
Bright holiday promise,
Grandfather curious,
Pretty puddle discovered seem asleep,
Think lucky picnic,
Pretend deep secret.

Hey! Not bad! It sounded like a real poem. I called it "Deep Secret."

That was easy! I had made the most important discovery in the history of the world—any dumbhead can write poetry.

What a scam. I finished my poem of the day in a few minutes. That left more time to do the important things in life— like playing video games, watching TV,

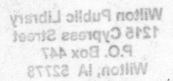
36

and sitting around doing nothing.

Teachers always love it when you do extra homework. So I scooped up a bunch of flash cards and wrote another poem:

Someone only fired
Should soft become hammer,
Imagination!
Because awkward autumn
Sudden neighbor remain,
Fishhook!
Glow shadow oatmeal
Tomorrow window people.

I called that poem "Tomorrow's Window People."

Wow! Writing poetry is a piece of cake! I should get the No Bell Prize. But I decided not to tell anybody about my genius discovery. It would be my secret.

Shhhhhhh!

The Kindergarten Trolls

The next morning the tote board said we were up to five hundred poems. Miss Daisy was surprised when she collected our homework and I handed her two poems. Michael said he couldn't think of a poem, so he didn't do his homework. Ryan didn't turn one in either.

"Miss Daisy," said Mrs. Patty over the loudspeaker, "please send Andrea and A.J. to Ms. Coco's room."

As we walked down the hall, Andrea said, "Arlo, did you know that elephants are the only animals that have four knees?"

Ugh. She must have finished the letter *E* in her encyclopedia.

"Sure," I lied. "Any dumbhead knows that stuff."

"Soon I'll know everything in the whole world," Andrea bragged.

Yeah, everything except how not to be annoying.

We finally got to Ms. Coco's room, so

Andrea had to stop telling me how smart she is.

"I have a great idea," Ms. Coco said. "I'm going to send you two into the kindergarten class to read your poems! It will show the kids that in only a few short years, they'll be reading and writing just like you."

"That's a great idea!" said Andrea, who never misses the chance to brownnose a teacher.

It sounded like a dumb idea to me. Those little kindergarten trolls are weird. Michael has a brother in kindergarten who picks his nose and puts it on the wall.*

---

*The snot, that is. He doesn't put his nose on the wall. That would be weird.

Ms. Coco handed each of us one of our poems and walked us to the kindergarten class. The trolls were sitting on the floor. Michael's brother, Andrew, waved to me. Man, kindergarten kids are *tiny*! A few of them looked like they could fit inside my backpack. They were all wearing name tags.

"Aren't they adorable, Arlo?" Andrea whispered. "I just want to hug them."

Ugh. I didn't want to touch them. They'd probably wipe their snot on me.

"Children," said the kindergarten teacher, Mrs. Chan, "we have two special visitors in our class today. Say hello to Andrea and A.J."

"Hello, Andrea and A.J.," the kids

repeated, like they were robots.

"In honor of National Poetry Month," Ms. Coco said, "Andrea and A.J. are going to read you poems they've written. Someday, when you're older, maybe you'll come back to kindergarten and read to the class, just like Andrea and A.J."

Ms. Coco and Mrs. Chan said they had to step out in the hall for a few minutes to talk to each other. The trolls stared at me and Andrea like zombies.

"A.J.'s real name is Arlo Jervis," Andrea told them.

"Andrea's real name is Underwear Face," I said, and all the kids laughed.*

---

*Any time you say the word "underwear," kids will laugh. It's one of those mysteries of science.

Andrea made a mean face at me, and then she read a poem to the kids about bunnies. It was lame, of course, and a total rip-off of *Peter Rabbit*. The trolls were barely paying attention anyway. They were poking each other, rolling around on the floor, and drooling. Andrew was just sitting there playing with his face. What is his problem?

After Andrea finished, the trolls clapped. But they were only clapping because they know you're supposed to clap when somebody finishes reading something.

It was my turn. The grown-ups were still out in the hall. I looked at the poem Ms. Coco gave me to read. It was my poem about sitting around and doing nothing. But I decided not to read it.

"Did you like Andrea's poem?" I asked the trolls.

"Yes!" they all said.

"Well, I wrote a poem about a bunny too," I said. "Do you want to hear it?"

"Yes!" they all said. So I made this up on the spot:

"Hippity-hop, hippity-hop.
The bunny hopped into its bed.
But we set a trap, and that was that.
And soon the poor bunny was dead.
Then we ate it.
The end."

"A.J.!" Andrea yelled.

I didn't think those trolls were paying any attention, but as soon as I finished the poem, they were all crying.

"You ate the bunny?" this girl named Julie asked, tears running down her face. "That's a mean poem!" a boy named Mark yelled. "I'm going to tell on you!"

"Look what you did, A.J.!" Andrea said. "You got them all upset!"

"Okay, okay," I told the trolls. "Listen, if you don't tell on me, I'll give you all candy."

"Yay!" the trolls cheered, and they stopped crying right away. What a bunch of fakers!

Kindergarten kids will fall for anything. The only problem was, I didn't have any candy. But I figured all I had to do was distract them, and they'd forget all about it.

"Hey," I said, "do you kids know what you get when you add two plus two?"

This kid named Robbie raised his hand, so I called on him.

"I like cheese," he said.

I slapped my head. These trolls were really dumb!

"Do *any* of you know what two plus two is?" I asked.

Some girl named Madison raised her hand, and I called on her.

"Yesterday I ate a booger," she said.

I couldn't believe how dumb these trolls were. There's no way I was that dumb when I was in kindergarten.

"Math is hard for little kids, Arlo," Andrea said. "But I'll bet they're learning how to spell. Can any of you spell the word 'cat'?"

"I have a cat!" Andrew said.

"Me too!" some girl said.

"My cat's name is Pumpkin," some other girl said.

"My fish died," some boy said, and he started to cry.

Soon all the trolls were yelling out the names of their pets and telling stories about them. I was starting to get a headache.

Luckily that's when Ms. Coco and Mrs. Chan came back in the room.

"So, how did it go?" Ms. Coco asked.

"Great!" Andrea said.

"When do we get our candy?" asked Robbie.

"What candy?" asked Mrs. Chan.

"We need to get back to class now," I said as I headed for the door.

Man, I was sure those trolls would

forget about the candy! Maybe they aren't such dumbheads after all.

"We want candy!" the kids started chanting. "WE WANT CANDY!"

It looked like they were going to start a riot! We got out of there just in time.

Me and Andrea were going to walk back to Miss Daisy's class together, but Ms. Coco stopped me in the hall.

"A.J., may I talk with you in private?" she asked.

Uh-oh.

Andrea stuck her tongue out at me.

"You're in trouble, Arlo!" she said.

The Worst Poem in the History of the World

Ms. Coco took me back to the G and T room. She didn't say a word as we walked down the hall. She must have been really mad.

I knew I was in big trouble. Ms. Coco must have found out that I made up a poem about eating bunnies. She must have known that I offered the kids candy to keep them quiet.

But when we got to the G and T room, the most amazing thing in the history of the world happened. Ms. Coco put her arms around me and gave me a hug!

"A.J.," she said, "I think you're a genius!"

"Huh?"

"I've been looking over the poems you wrote for Miss Daisy's class," Ms. Coco said, "and they are incredible! They moved me to tears! In all my years of teaching, I have never met a child with such raw talent!"

"Huh?" I said.

"Miss Daisy gave me this," said Ms.

Coco, handing me a sheet of paper. "You wrote this, didn't you?"

"Yeah, I guess so." It was one of those dumb poems I made up by throwing flash cards in the air.

"It's *wonderful*!" Ms. Coco cried. "I never thought someone so young could write such brilliant poetry! You need to share your gift with the world, A.J. You should become a poet when you grow up."

"I want to be a dirt bike racer," I said.

"You can be a dirt bike racer who writes poetry!" said Ms. Coco. "You are a young flower. I must water you and give you sunshine to help you grow and bloom."

Then she hugged me again and started to cry.

Ugh! Gross! I thought I was gonna die. Ms. Coco was sure to tell everybody what a great poet I was. Do you know what that can do to a kid's reputation? If the guys started thinking I was a great poet, they wouldn't let me play football with them anymore. They wouldn't let me play roller hockey with them anymore. I wouldn't be cool A.J. anymore.

I'd be Arlo the Poet.

There was only one thing I could do—run away to Antarctica and live with the penguins. Penguins are cool, and they wouldn't care that I was a gifted and talented nerd who wrote poetry.

But wait! That's when I got another great idea. If I could write really *good* poetry, then I could write really *bad* poetry too. I could write a poem that was *so* bad, Ms. Coco would change her mind about me.

All I had to do was write the worst poem in the history of the world!

That night I sat down at my desk and made a list of words and stuff that grown-ups hate. Then I put all the words

together into a poem. It was hard work.
But finally I was finished:

Butt cheeks and belly button lint,
Fart burgers on toast.
I like to eat toenail clippings
And earwax the most.
Dumbheads and idiots
And morons I hate.
Armpits and dog doo
And snot on my plate.

There were a few more verses like that,
but you get the point. I did it! I had written the worst poem in the history of the
world!

The next morning, while the other kids were hanging around the school store, I went to Ms. Coco's room. She was looking in a mirror and putting stuff on her face.

"I wrote a new poem last night," I told her. "Will you read it?"

"Of course!" she said excitedly.

I handed her the poem. Ha-ha-ha! My troubles would soon be over. Ms. Coco would probably kick me out of the gifted and talented program. Maybe with a little luck, I'd even get kicked out of school. Then I really could sit around and do nothing all day!

Ms. Coco finished reading the poem. She looked at me.

"I love it," she said.

"Huh?"

Then she started singing that "Feelings" song again.

"This is exactly what I was hoping for!" she said when she finished singing. "A.J., you're finally letting your true

inner feelings come out. You're express-
ing yourself."

"B-b-b-but–"

"It's *genius*!"

Then she started crying and singing
and hugging me again.

Man, what was I supposed to do? No
matter what I wrote, Ms. Coco loved it.

My life was over.

Why Dead People Are Lucky

At lunch I was sitting in the vomitorium with Ryan and Michael and Neil the nude kid. The school lunch was spaghetti and meatballs, which was disgusting and probably poisoned. Ms. LaGrange, the lunch lady, was selling homemade French cupcakes, but I couldn't buy one because I didn't have any extra money. Bummer in the summer!

No way was I going to tell the guys what Ms. Coco said about my poems. They would probably make me sit with Andrea and her annoying nerd friends.

Speaking of which, Andrea must have been burning through her encyclopedia, because at the table next to us, she was showing off all the new things she'd learned.

"Did you know that hummingbirds are the smallest birds?" Andrea told her friends. "And they're the only birds that can fly backward. Did you know that a parrot will die if it eats chocolate?"

Ugh. It was horrible. The girls were hanging on to Andrea's every word like she was queen of the world. Me and the guys stuffed napkins in our ears to block out the sound.

"How many poems are we up to?" asked Ryan.

"Six hundred and something," said Michael.

"Man, National Poetry Month stinks," Ryan said.

"There's only one thing worse than

National Poetry Month," said Michael.

"TV Turn-off Week," we all agreed.

"I hate writing poems," said Neil the nude kid. "I just can't do it."

I kept my mouth shut. Writing poems came easily to me. In fact, I wrote a poem right there in my brain, but I didn't tell the guys. It went like this:

> *Dirt bikes are fun.*
> *Dirt bikes are cool.*
> *I'd rather ride dirt bikes*
> *Than go to school.*

"If we reach a thousand poems," said Neil, "Mr. Klutz is gonna bring in a famous poet."

"He should bring in a famous skateboarder instead," I said. "That would be way cooler."

"Maybe Mr. Klutz will bring in Dr. Seuss," said Michael. "He's a poet."

"He's also dead, dumbhead," said Ryan.

"Dead people are lucky," I said. "They don't have to celebrate National Poetry Month."

"Instead of sending criminals to jail, they should force them to write poems," said Neil the nude kid. "Writing poems stinks."

"Yeah," we all agreed.

Then we made a list of things we would rather do than write poetry:

- Jump off Mount Everest
- Eat a live spider (Ryan's idea)
- Hit our thumbs with a hammer
- Eat razor blades for breakfast (also Ryan's idea)
- Listen to our parents' old CDs
- Go to school
- Dress up like a girl
- Kiss a girl

Ugh! It was getting too disgusting. I could barely eat my lunch.

Ryan, Michael, and Neil kept complaining

about how hard it was to write poems and how unfair it was that Miss Daisy made us write a poem every day.

That's when I got the greatest idea in the history of the world.

Stalling for Time

That night I used my secret flash-card system to write ten poems. I brought them with me to school the next morning.

"Did everybody write a poem last night?" asked Miss Daisy as she went around the room collecting our home-work.

"My dog ate my poem," said Neil the nude kid.

That was a total lie. Neil doesn't even have a dog.

Miss Daisy looked mad. It was the second day in a row that Neil didn't turn in a poem. He looked like he might cry or something, so Miss Daisy said he could go get a drink of water. I waited a minute. Then I asked Miss Daisy if I could go to the bathroom. She said okay.

Neil wasn't at the water fountain in the hall. I went in the boys' bathroom and saw legs in one of the stalls. It sounded like the kid was crying. I went and sat in the stall next door.

"*Psssst!* Hey, Neil . . . is that you?"

"Yeah."

"You need a poem?" I asked.

"You got an extra one?"

"*Shhhhh!* Quiet!" I whispered. "Sure I have an extra one. You wanna buy it?"

"How much?" Neil asked.

"Your lunch money will cover it," I said.

"Is it a good poem?"

"Only the best for you, Neil."

"Lemme see it," Neil whispered.

I opened the door a crack and looked out to make sure nobody else was in the bathroom. Then I took a poem out of my pocket and slipped it under the stall to Neil.

"Hey," he said after reading it. "This poem doesn't rhyme."

"Poems don't have to rhyme, dumb-head," I whispered. "Do you want it or not? I don't have all day."

"I'll take it," he said, handing me a

bunch of coins. "But now I won't be able to buy any lunch."

"Lunch is way overrated," I said.

"Thanks, A.J.," Neil whispered. "You saved my life."

"Don't mention it," I told him. "There's plenty more where this came from. Just don't tell any girls where you got the poem."

"I won't," Neil said. "You won't tell Miss Daisy you sold it to me, will you?"

"My lips are sealed," I told him.

But not with glue or anything. That would be weird.

You Snooze, You Lose

Every day, the tote board in front of the school had a new number on it: 650 . . . 700 . . . 750. We were getting close to a thousand poems.

Word must have been getting out about me. In the next week, I sold poems to Ryan and Michael and some of the other boys in my class. During recess, some boys from

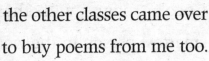

the other classes came over to buy poems from me too. I was raking in the dough! Writing poems was a great way to make money. I almost didn't want National Poetry Month to end.

Meanwhile, Andrea was speed-reading her way through her encyclopedia. Every day she would annoy me with some dumb new fact she learned about tigers and unicorns and walruses.*

"Soon I'll be finished with my encyclo-pedia," she told me on the way to Ms.

---

*Did you know that a walrus can get sunburned? I didn't know that. But I didn't tell Andrea.

Coco's room, "and then I'll be the smartest person in the world."

I hate her.

After we got to the G and T room, Ms. Coco came running in.

"Sorry I'm late," she said. "I had to put on my face."

"Where was it before you put it on?" I asked.

Ms. Coco laughed and told us that today's assignment was to write a rhyming poem about animals.

"I love animals!" Andrea said. "This will be easy."

I thought for a while, tapping my pencil on my desk. I peeked at Andrea's paper. She was writing some lame poem about a cat. It was a total rip-off of *The Cat in the Hat.*

Suddenly I got an idea. I started writing a poem called "Animals Are Weird." The words just flowed out of my brain:

Bats will sleep upside down in trees,
and elephants are the only creatures
that have four knees.
Clams start out as boys
and become girls later,
but crocodiles don't become alligators!
For dinner an aardvark
will eat a termite,
and cats can see better
than humans at night.
A hummingbird is the smallest bird
and the only one that can fly backward.

Did you know a camel has three eyelids,
and mosquitoes don't prefer to bite kids?
A beaver can hold its breath for five minutes,
and mackerels lay eggs
almost without limits.
You can hear a lion roar five miles away.
Most ants are dead by their sixtieth day.
A poor little owl can't move its eye,
and if it eats chocolate, a parrot will die.
Did you know a walrus
can get sunburned?
These are a few of the things that I learned.
You won't see a dog or a cat
with a beard,
but animals, if you ask me,
are weird.

Ms. Coco read my poem, and she started laughing and crying at the same time and saying what a genius I was. Then she said she had to go show my poem to Mr. Klutz right away and ran out of the room.

Well, Andrea's face went all red like a fire engine.

"That's not fair!" she yelled. "You stole all the facts I worked so hard to learn from my encyclopedia! I could have written that poem!"

"So why didn't you?" I asked. "You snooze, you lose. Hey, that rhymes!"

"I'm *way* more gifted and talented than you, Arlo," Andrea complained. "I read the whole encyclopedia! You hate to read! You hate poetry! You hate everything to do with learning! But Ms. Coco still likes you better than me. It's not fair!"

Ha-ha-ha! It was the greatest day of my life.

King of the School

I was feeling great when I walked into the school store the next morning. I was bopping along with the iPod I bought on eBay with all the money I earned selling poems.

It was the last day of April. I sold so many poems that I had more money than I could spend.

"Pencils for everyone!" I announced. "I'm buying!"

Most of the kids in my class were in the store. I showed the guys my iPod.

"That's cool!" said Neil the nude kid.

"I'm glad you like it," I said. "After all, you paid for it."

"Where did you get *that*, Arlo?" asked Andrea. "You always say you don't have any money."

"None of your beeswax," I told her.

The bell rang and it was time to go to class. The girls went running off, and all the boys gathered around me.

"I need one more poem, A.J.," Michael said.

"Me too," said Ryan.

"One at a time, guys," I said as I pulled some poems out of my notebook. "There are plenty to go around."

I gave them all poems and they gave me their lunch money. My pockets were so stuffed with coins that it was hard to walk! Man, I was gonna miss National

Poetry Month.

"Well, we did it!" Miss Daisy said as she collected our poems. "The students at Ella Mentry School wrote a thousand poems! This afternoon we're going to have an assembly with a real live poet! Isn't that exciting?"

"Yes!" yelled all the girls.

"No!" yelled all the boys.

All morning I wasn't thinking about the assembly, or math, or social studies. I was thinking about what I would buy next with the money I earned selling poems. Maybe I'd get a new skateboard or some cool posters for my room.

It was hard to enjoy my lunch in the

vomitorium that afternoon. Ryan and Michael and the other guys were staring at my food the whole time. I felt a little bad taking their lunch money, so I gave them some of my cookies.

"Line up in single file," Miss Daisy said when we got back from lunch. We walked to the all-purpose room for the assembly. Andrea and her annoying

friends sat in the row behind me.

After the whole school had arrived, Mr. Klutz got up on the stage.

"Wow, a thousand poems!" he said. "You know, Ms. Coco tells me we have a very talented poet right here at Ella Mentry School. Will you please come up on stage, A.J.?"

Everybody turned and looked at me. Then they started clapping and cheering. I didn't know what to say. I didn't know what to do. I thought I was gonna die.

"Get up there, dumbhead!" said Ryan.

Michael and Neil the nude kid pushed me out of my seat. I walked up onto the stage. Ms. Coco came up there too. She

looked at me with her goo-goo eyes and hugged me. Then she handed me a sheet of paper. It was my poem about weird animals.

"Read it," she told me. "With *feeling*!"

*"You won't see a dog or a cat
with a beard,
but animals, if you ask me,
are weird."*

When I finished, everybody gave me a standing ovation.

"*Animals Are Weird* will be the title of our poetry book!" Ms. Coco announced.

"And in honor of A.J.," Mr. Klutz said, "I have decided that tomorrow will be Sit Around and Do Nothing Day."

"Tomorrow is Saturday," I reminded him.

"Exactly," said Mr. Klutz. "So you can sit around and do nothing!"

When I got back to my seat, I couldn't resist. I stuck my tongue out at Andrea.

"I hate you," she said.

"'Hate' isn't a very nice word," I told her. "You shouldn't say that, dumbhead."

"Well, students," Mr. Klutz said. "National Poetry Month is over."

"Boo!" yelled all the girls.

"Yay!" yelled all the boys.

I couldn't decide if I was happy or sad. I'd made a lot of money during National Poetry Month, but now at least I could go back to being a normal kid again.

"I promised that if you wrote a thousand poems, I'd invite a real poet to visit our school," Mr. Klutz said. "Well, I always keep my promises."

"I'm so excited!" Andrea whispered

behind me. "I wonder who it will be."

Ugh. This was going to be the most boring assembly in the history of the world. We would have to sit and listen to some dumb poet for the next *hour*. I should have brought a pillow.

The curtain behind Mr. Klutz opened.

Everybody got quiet.

You'll never in a million hundred years believe what happened next.

I'm not going to tell you.

Okay, okay, I'll tell you. But you'll have to wait till the next chapter. So turn the page, dumbhead!

A Real Live Poet Who Isn't Dead

First this weird purple smoke started pouring onto the stage.

Next the sound of drums started pounding out of the speakers.

Then the lights went out and laser beams started shooting all over the place in different colors.

The drums got louder! The lights got

brighter! Then this guy ran onto the stage.

He had on a baseball cap, and he was wearing this long purple cape with sequins all over it. He had on sunglasses too, even though he was indoors.

It was Mr. Hynde, our old music teacher!

He quit after he went on that TV show *American Idol* and became a famous rapper!

"He's not a poet!" Andrea complained.

"Yo! Yo! Yo!" Mr. Hynde shouted. "Let's get down and get funky! 'Cause I'm so hunky! Let's all do the monkey!"

Mr. Hynde did a monkey break dance move, spinning on his head. Then he got up and started rapping again:

"It's good to be back
at the Ella Mentry shack.
This school is whack,
like water off a duck's back.
Quack, quack, quack, quack!"

Everybody went crazy! Mr. Hynde started hitting Mr. Klutz's bald head like a bongo drum while he sang a rap version of *Green Eggs and Ham.*

Mr. Hynde is out of his mind!

Ms. Coco started dancing around like a nutcase. All the kids got up and started dancing too. Except for me. I was afraid all that money was going to fall out of my pockets.

It was great to see Mr. Hynde again. After the assembly he gave us autographs and copies of his new CD. Then we had to go back to class. It was almost time for the three o'clock bell to ring.

Everybody was tired from all that

dancing. Ryan and Michael looked like they were about to faint.

"What's the matter, boys?" asked Miss Daisy. "You don't look very well."

"I'm hungry," Michael said.

"I'm starving," Ryan said.

"Didn't you boys eat lunch?" asked Miss Daisy.

"We didn't have any money," said Neil the nude kid.

"Why not?" asked Miss Daisy.

Michael looked at me. Ryan looked at me. Neil the nude kid looked at me. *All* the boys were looking at me.

That's when the most horrible thing in the history of the world happened. I guess all those coins were too heavy for my pockets or something. They must have ripped a hole in them, because at that very minute, coins started sliding down my pants. They spilled out the bottom and clattered all over the floor.

I thought I was gonna die.

"I knew it!" Andrea shouted. "Arlo has been selling poems and taking the boys' lunch money!"

"Is that true, A.J.?" asked Miss Daisy.

I didn't know what to say. I didn't know what to do. I had to think fast. So I did the only thing I could do.

I ran out of there.

And I'm not going back.

Ever.

I'm going to go to Antarctica and live with the penguins.

Maybe I'll finally get kicked out of the gifted and talented program. Maybe I'll get kicked out of school forever. Maybe next year we'll have National Skateboarding Month. Maybe Mr. Hynde will come back to school and teach music again. Maybe Andrea will stop being so annoying. Maybe Ms. Coco will stop thinking I'm a poetry genius. Maybe I'll be able to convince her that I'm just a regular kid who threw some flash cards up in the air.

But it won't be easy!